James Howard Kunstler

The Law of the Jungle

A Tale of Loss and Woe

———————

ALSO BY JAMES HOWARD KUNSTLER

Fiction

A Safe and Happy Place

The World Made By Hand Series
The Harrows of Spring
A History of the Future
The Witch of Hebron
World Made By Hand

Maggie Darling, a Modern Romance
Thunder Island
The Halloween Ball
The Hunt
Blood Solstice
An Embarrassment of Riches
The Life of Byron Jaynes
A Clown in the Moonlight
The Wampanaki Tales.

Nonfiction

Too Much Magic
The Long Emergency
The City in Mind
Home From Nowhere
The Geography of Nowhere

James Howard Kunstler

The Law of the Jungle

A Tale of Loss and Woe

A Novella

The Greenaway Series
Book Five

Highbrow Press

Published in the United States of America

ISBN 13: 978-1987706246

Highbrow Press
PO Box 193
Saratoga Springs
New York, 12866

Long ago — at least half a century —
when mastodons roamed the boreal uplands of
Vermont, and the commodious Checker cab
ruled the streets of Manhattan, and President
Kennedy met with leaders of newly-minted
tropical nations who wore bone ornaments in
their facial parts, a twelve-year-old boy named
Jeff Greenaway was sent away from home for the
full eight-week summer session to Camp
Timahoe, as had been the case for five previous
summers.

Camp Timahoe, a boys-only
establishment, was located in a particularly
remote northeastern quadrant of the Green
Mountain State eleven miles away from the mill
town of Lost Indian. Getting there required an
overnight sleeper train ride from Grand Central
Station 320 miles clear up to St. Johnsbury, near
the Canadian border, and then, the next morning,
an additional hour ride in the old war surplus
army truck that was the camp's main bulk
conveyance for boys.

Camp Timahoe was the life project of the
magnetic Murray Horvath, who bought the
eighty-acre parcel in the depths of the Great
Depression from a distressed Utopian religious
group called the Brothers of the Practical Arts.
They had gone broke making luxury wooden
furniture in the manner of William Morris, their

1

specialty being the rather high-priced chair they called the Lumbar Hygiene Recliner.

If you suppose for a moment that Jeff Greenaway was despondent about being cast out of his home on 79th Street for two months you would be most mistaken. In fact, he was delirious to be shipped off to "the country," which was his mother's term for any place where you could not buy a Charlotte Russe inside a five-minute walk. He barely tolerated the city during the cold months of the year, with its meager offerings of activities for boys — the natural history museum, the planetarium, the Central Park Zoo, the movies — and to him the very idea of a whole summer in the city was like unto a term in the penitentiary, even a kind of premature death.

The things that interested Jeff were the things that boys from time immemorial like to do: swim on hot days, catch fish on sultry evenings, explore the darkling woods, play the various games that involve balls and running on grass — exactly the things unavailable in a city designed strictly for grownups, with their boring restaurants and nauseating Broadway shows. Jeff also had a complete set of summer camp friends separate from his city school friends, children who had come up through the bunks with him since age seven, most of whom lived in various suburban outlands of the city — for instance, Paul "Goose" Gosdorfer of Great Neck, Long Island, Marvin "Buddy" Wollenreich, of Bedford,

Westchester County, and Steve "Soul Brother Number One (or SB)" Schlossmeyer of New Canaan, Connecticut. Unbeknownst to his parents or school friends, Jeff was known at Camp Timahoe almost exclusively by his own summer moniker, "Ace."

Now it happened that the camp season began auspiciously. The train ride north was especially fun since Goose managed to smuggle aboard an empty shampoo bottle filled with his father's gin, lending a riotous edge to the squirt-gun battles that raged up and down the two chartered Pullman cars. And when that was over they devoured the two-pound bag of Hershey's Miniatures that SB had appropriated from the family snack drawer. (And then they fell asleep in their berths.)

The next day, following the truck ride and grand arrival, during the ceremonial first day pancake breakfast and reading of bunk assignments, "the Four Horsemen of the Campocalypse" — Goose, Buddy, SB, and Ace — were promoted into the lofty ranks of the "senior" campers, who had their own grove of cabins separate from the irksome "intermediates" and the loathsome "juniors." The counselor assigned to their cabin (Bunk 9) was the chief of the waterfront staff, the dashing and humorous Tom "Bushcat" Kroger, a senior at the University of Vermont and holder of the then-current NCAA record for the 200-yard backstroke ("almost an Olympian," Murray Horvath liked to brag to parents' when he described the staff).

Being seniors also came with some responsibilities and perquisites. Seniors could wear long pants (khakis) if they felt like it instead of the mandatory red-and-green shorts of the younger boys. Seniors acted as waiters in the camp dining room, rotating around the tables in pairs every other day so they got to enjoy the company of the more entertaining counselors, who sat at the head of each table. As compensation for lugging the trays of oatmeal and Salisbury steak and Fudgsicles back and forth, Murray took all eighteen waiters into Lost Indian every Thursday night, where they could go to either the teen street dance on one blocked-off side of the square, or go to the movies in the dilapidated "opera house" catty-cornered to the dance on the other side.

As early as the Fourth of July, the first sign appeared that something was not quite right this season at Camp Timahoe. As usual, Murray trucked all the boys over to Lost Indian to see the annual fireworks show. But on the way into the fairgrounds, Murray got in "an altercation" (it was said later) with the parking lot attendant that drew the attention of two county sheriff's deputies, on duty there to guard against teen necking and other threats to public safety. Ultimatums were issued by both the deputies ("jail!") and Murray ("lawsuit!"). Murray eventually forked over an entry fee based on collective occupancy of the truck at ten cents a head (instead of the old dollar-per-vehicle of previous years). For days afterward, Murray would refer to the incident as "literally highway robbery." He could be heard muttering "greedy bastards" as he shuffled in and out of his office in the lodge — the old furniture factory that now served as Camp Timahoe's general headquarters, game room, and eating place.

The next sign of trouble occurred a week later when Murray administered the morning allergy shots to the several boys who needed them, in place of the camp nurse, Maxine, who happened to be Mrs. Horvath, and who had actually not appeared for meals or been seen around the property since the Fourth of July. At supper that Sunday night, Murray announced that Nurse Maxine had been constrained suddenly to travel to Frenchtown, New Jersey, to care for an elderly aunt "stricken with acute crepuscular lumbago," he said, and might not return until later in the season. Eyebrows were raised among the counselors at the heads of the tables, who had seen evidence of Maxine's drinking.

In another ominous development that same night, Virgil the dishwasher, an aspiring auto mechanic studying at the Vermont State School of Vocations and Trades, was "absent

5

without leave," as Murray put it delicately. And so a crew was drafted from the highest bunk (No. 13) with the most mature campers to do his job until the formerly diligent native of Lost Indian could be located. The boys were promised double rations at the Tuesday candy canteen.

Three evenings after that, in the interval before lights out, at the beginning of a heat wave, with mosquitoes, crane flies, and moths infiltrating the tattered screens of Bunk 9 and then whirring disgustingly around the single bare bulb hanging at the center of the cabin, Tom Kroger gathered the Four Horsemen around his footlocker for "an important meeting."

"What's up, Bushcat?" Ace asked. "Want to borrow another ten bucks from us?" The counselor was known to be carrying on an expensive romance with a Lost Indian girl named Rhonda-Jean, renowned for her bosomy "balcony," who waitressed at the A & W Root Beer stand on the edge of town.

"Not exactly, " Kroger said, appearing to struggle with what he had to say.

"Watch," SB said. "He's gonna hit us for twenty now."

"Is anybody here not a wise guy?" Kroger asked.

The four all glanced at each other.

"I don't think so," Buddy spoke for all of them.

"Anyway, you still haven't paid us back since last time," SB said.

"Yeah, well...." Kroger trailed off, and then held up a sheaf of paper papers. "You see these?"

"How can you miss them," Goose said. "They're right in our face?"

"Do you want to do ten minutes of Iron Cross, Gosdorfer?" Kroger asked. At Camp Timahoe, the use of last names in personal address was always ominous. The Iron Cross, a traditional punishment for wise guys, did not actually involve anything iron, but rather the holding out of heavy rocks in a crucifixion-like posture until the deltoid muscles collapsed in exhaustion. The name Iron Cross was attached simply to invoke the Nazis, those exemplars of sadism, not long ago crushed by the allied forces of democracy and decency.

"No," Goose said.

"Then let's cut the clowning-around, huh?" Kroger said. He dealt out the papers to the Four Horseman like playing cards on top of the foot-locker, with a contemptuous flick of the wrist for each one. They picked them up. "These are your junior life-saver certifications," he said.

"But we only just started the training two weeks ago," Ace said.

"You'll keep taking it, but you're gonna have to watch over the juniors and intermediates down at the lake during free swim."

"Huh?" Buddy said. "How come."

"'Cuz two of my other waterfront counselors aren't going to be around anymore."

"Where'd they go?"

"They quit," Kroger said.

"Why?" Goose asked.

"That's classified information," Kroger said.

"But when do we get to swim?" Ace asked.

"We'll figure that out later," Kroger said. "In the meantime, take your responsibilities seriously."

"Do we get anything for it?" SB asked.

"No, you're doing it for the glory," Kroger said. "But you can keep the light on an extra half hour from now on. Oh, by the way, Murray told us to tell you not to seal the envelopes of your letters to home anymore.

"Huh...?" Ace said.

"Say, what?" said SB.

"What's he checking for?" Buddy said. "Moose turds?"

"Don't look at me," Kroger said. "I don't make the rules around here."

"I'm gonna write a letter saying Nurse Maxine tried to get me to do the deed with her last year up in the office," Goose said. "See what happens."

"Oh, that's a great idea," Tom Kroger said, rolling his eyes.

As it happened, two of the oldest boys from Bunk 13, Alan Hufnagel and Bob Skurtz, were drafted to take over for the two counselors who had so suddenly and mysteriously quit. They were assigned to sleep in intermediate bunks 3 and 6 where the younger boys required supervision before lights out and during cleanup and rest period, and in some cases, to tie their shoes in the morning. In the dining room, they reverted to being waiters, while the abandoned head seats of two tables remained conspicuously vacant. Murray designated Hufnagel and Skurtz as "counselors-in-training," intimating that they were not paid positions, but would confer on the older boys a reward of "premature maturity and manliness." Other "opportunities" might open up before the season was over, he concluded, but before he could sit down to his plate of "train wreck," as the traditional Wednesday night macaroni and hamburger dish was known, a hand went up.

"What do you mean 'opportunities?'" Ace blurted out when Murray tried to ignore him.

"I'm not taking any questions, Murray said, with an actorish smile. "But since you asked, I mean the chance to rise in the ranks, son, to become... as men."

"But we're still kids," SB said.

"You're aware, are you not," Murray said, "that some years ago this country had to fight the Nazis and the Japs, both at the same time?"

A murmur of general agreement rose among the tables.

"Yeah, World War Two," Goose explained.

"Correct," Murray said. "In those dark days, boys became men overnight. They had to. It was kill or be killed. My kid brother Jules was one of them: fifteen when the Gerries invaded Poland, small for his age, a skinny beanpole, not much bigger than Greenaway over there. But four years later he was marching toward Palermo, Sicily, a machine gun hanging over his shoulder, following the glorious footsteps of General George Patton, the greatest field commander on our side, a giant amongst men. Of course, it wasn't the General's fault that Jules got killed on the docks at Messina three weeks later when a broken cargo crane fell on him... goddammit" — Murray said, tearing up as he always did when speaking of long lost Jules — "but they gave him the purple heart post-humorously. He came into the war a boy but died a man. Did I answer your question, Greenaway?"

"I think so," Ace said. "What did you do in the war, sir?"

"I had an acute recess of the posterior myopia," Murray said. "It affected my balance. To this day I can't stand on one leg in the dark. The army wouldn't take me. By then, of course, I'd already acquired this place and youngsters were coming here from the city, establishing the great Timahoe traditions and defending the home front. We kept our eyes on the sky for enemy aircraft sneaking in over Canada. We saved big balls of twine for the war effort and planted victory gardens. We didn't get any meat until after VJ Day. So count your blessings, son."

Ace nodded and returned to his seat as a solemn silence came over the room. Murray declared the whole camp could have seconds of fudgsicles that evening, and the candy canteen was unexpectedly opened after supper as well.

"Hey Bushcat," Ace asked the Bunk 9 counselor later that evening after the recorded bugle tattoo played over the loudspeaker in the second floor window of the Lodge, sending all the boys down the hill to their cabins. "Are we at war?"

Tom Kroger stared back at Ace as if he was insane.

"Where'd you get that idea?"

"Weird things are happening around here," Ace said. "People are vanishing."

"Yeah, well, you know, sometimes people vanish," Kroger said and reached for his copy of *Atlas Shrugged*.

""No they don't," Ace said. "Not here. Every other year they just stuck around. Maybe they're running off to join the army."

"There's no war on, Ace."

"How do you know?"

Kroger, who was now supine on his "rack" (i.e. cot) next to Ace's cot, placed the paperback book on his stomach.

"Lookit," he said. "What's on the radio right now?"

It happened that Goose's titanic eight-battery Zenith portable was tuned into WBZ Boston, and just then the station was playing Ray Steven's giant hit, *Ahab the Arab*.

"So...?" Ace said.

"You don't think they'd be playing the top ten if we were at war, do you?"

"I dunno...."

"They'd be broadcasting the civil defense, telling everybody to go to their bomb shelters," Kroger said. "Anyway, if we were at war, who would it be with?"

"The Russians?"

"Right, the Russians. And you know what that would be like?"

"Atom bombs...?"

"Of course, atom bombs," Kroger said. "Talk about people vanishing! Like in ten seconds: *phhhhtttt*, five hundred million dead, just like that."

"So why are they vanishing?"

"Hey, you got to pay people. Now, do you mind if I get a little reading in?"

"He's not paying them?" Ace asked.

"Like I said," Kroger said, finally propping his book back up. "You got to pay people."

The next evening, after a postprandial softball game in the long, lingering July twilight, the Four Horsemen returned to discover a most disquieting situation in Bunk 9. Tom Kroger's footlocker, indeed all his effects, were missing.

"Holy jumping Jeezus," Buddy said. "Bushcat got sucked out of the universe too."

"What do we do now?" SB said.

It was just then that the Camp Timahoe director himself, Murray Horvath, stepped through the bunk door with its musically creaky spring, without knocking.

"Hello boys," he said, his customary smile subdued, his fine head of silver hair slightly disheveled, as if he'd been massaging his head in his office. He strode to the center of the cabin and sat on the end of SB's bed. "Come gather round, guys."

The Four Horsemen sat on the remaining footlockers.

"Gee, Murray," SB said. "What happened to Bushcat... er, Tom?"

"His mother came down with hypothetical craniofacial syndrome," Murray replied gravely. "I had to let him go home."

"Everybody's disappearing," Ace said. "It's weird."

"Don't worry, son. Next year I'll require medical clearance for all employees," Murray said. "It's true, the attrition has been deplorable.

But with a little extra help from you older fellows, I believe we'll get through this rough patch just fine. Which brings me to the point. I'm forming a special group of the older boys, one from each of the senior bunks, a Council of Elders, so to speak, to help me manage the, uh, ongoing situation. Greenaway, you've been nominated to represent this bunk."

"Who nominated me?"

"The nominating committee."

"Sir," Goose said, "Greenaway's not mentally stable."

"Who says?" Murray asked.

"Bushcat said so all the time."

"He said the same thing about all of us," Ace said.

"Son," Murray said, "Tom was a man of harsh and extreme opinions. It's what made him such a great leader. I've known all of you since you were pups. Watched you rise through the ranks. I think I'm a good judge of character and I don't think any of you belong in the state hospital. Well, maybe Gosdorfer would get something out of seeing a psychiatrist."

Three of the Four Horsemen tittered at that. Murray waved off the joke.

"These are times that will test the Camp Timahoe spirit," he continued, "and I know that I can depend on you." He reached into his jacket pocket and pulled out a handful of Bit'o'Honey miniatures. "Here. Fortify yourselves for the days

14

ahead. First meeting of the Council of Elders is tomorrow after breakfast, Greenaway."

"What do we do without a counselor?" Buddy asked as Murray stood up.

"How long have you been a Timahoe boy, Marvin?"

"Six years."

"Think you've learned the routine by now?"

"I guess."

"Well, I'm gonna go up to the lodge in a little while and put *Taps* on over the old PA. You know what *Taps* means, don't you?"

"Yes, sir."

"And then, when the sun comes back up, I put on *Reveille*, right? And what do you do then?"

"We get up?"

"Exactly! See? You fellows are good learners. You'll do fine on your own."

Murray strode back to the door. This time, the spring sounded like the shriek of *Rodan the Flying Reptile* when he flew out of the Japanese volcano to begin his career of mayhem and terror.

"Good night, men," Murray said.

"Some of you may have noticed the staff difficulties we've had this season," Murray began the extraordinary meeting of the Council of Elders after a breakfast of nothing but cold cereal — no eggs, no pancakes, no French toast, which comprised the usual rotation of entrees for the morning meal. "I've never seen so many people with medical problems like this bunch. The latest victim, I'm sorry to say, is Gerald the cook. He's been here with us since, gosh, the Korean War, and was struck down just after dawn's early light with fungal congestion of the esophageal myotis. We think it was from a batch of bad pinto beans in last night's chili—"

"How come none of us got infected?" Russell Holzinger of Bunk 12 asked.

"A good question," Murray said. "A very good question, indeed." Murray appeared to ponder and cogitate, and at length he explained: "Well, the doctor said that the particular organism lives in the airspace at the top of the can and is transmitted when opened by inhaling the fumes that contain the fungal spores. Apparently, the beans themselves are unaffected."

"Is he gonna make it?" asked Josh Sklar of Bunk 10.

"They're not sure," Murray said. "And to think we might never eat his meatloaf again. Gosh, I hope he gets through this. How about we say a little prayer for dear old Gerald now?"

"Like, the Kaddish?" asked Ricky Gendelman of Bunk 11.

"He's not dead yet, stupid," said Holzinger.

"A moment of silence will do," Murray said.

When the twenty seconds or so was over, Murray had a few more announcements. Until further notice, lunch and supper would be held at the cookout patch, as it was called, between the intermediate and senior groves of bunks. Traditionally, cookout night was Tuesday, Gerald's one weekly night off. And traditionally — meaning as far back as anyone could remember — the procedure involved cooking scores of frankfurters in a 15-gallon restaurant-grade stockpot over a wood-fired fieldstone barbeque. Campers could eat as many dogs as they wanted, and high status was conferred on those who could hold down four, buns included. The traditional side dish, for ease of service, was potato chips. The usual condiments were offered. Murray himself volunteered to be in charge of the operation.

Next, Murray announced that the last of the counselors, Helmut (arts and crafts) and Werner (archery), two foreign students studying at Middlebury College, had departed for home that morning due to a new political flare-up in Berlin over the recently constructed wall between East and West.

Murray briskly set forth a plan in which the senior campers would be assigned duties and roles for the rest of the season to replace the departed counselors. More seniors, like Hufnagel and Skurtz, would have to sleep in the bunks of the younger boys. Some seniors were assigned to run particular activities: boating, swim instruction, baseball, tennis, etc.

"How about riflery," Ace Greenaway inquired. "I could run that."

The older elders tittered and pointed at him.

"I could," Ace insisted.

"Sorry, son, that's on lockdown," Murray explained. "Ditto archery. But you can be on breakfast duty, you know, put out the cereal boxes and the milk pitchers. You can do that, right?"

"I guess," Ace said.

"What about our Thursday night out in town for the street-dance?" Holzinger asked anxiously. He had an interest in a Lost Indian high school freshman named Suzanne Brunelle who had turned up there a couple of weeks in a row. She spoke in the alluring accent of her family's native Quebec and was, Holzinger tirelessly repeated, "extremely well-developed."

"Well, there'll be some changes with that, too," Murray said. "Obviously, all you seniors can't go into town at once. At least half of you will have to stay here and hold down the fort, keep the youngsters busy, get them down the hill to bed, and so forth. So you'll split up into two teams, red and green, and alternate Thursday nights in town...."

A slight but discernable groan filled the room.

"Come on now, boys. Act like men! This is an emergency. The law of the jungle is in effect and the venerable Camp Timahoe project is in danger. You guys really have to help me out with this."

For the first time, Murray Horvath's luminous and charismatic demeanor seemed to dim slightly, while his sturdy physical frame visibly deflated. He slumped in his seat and heaved a sigh, staring emptily across the circle of chairs at Ace Greenaway, 180 degrees around the circle. Ace could barely stand to look into Murray's eyes. All the old fire had gone out in them.

"Oh, one other thing," Murray said in a much diminished vocal register. "I'm cancelling parents' weekend."

This was greeted with a mix of despair and jubilation. For instance, Holzinger's parents always brought up a giant box of gourmet snacks and candy, while Hufnagel would have been happy to stay at Camp Timahoe all winter, by himself, if necessary, and never see his parents again.

"We just can't chance it with any more illness around here," Murray continued. "God knows what they'd bring up from the city: polio, dropsy, the vapors."

"What's the vapors, Murray?" Skurtz inquired.

"Slow suffocation, like drowning in poison mist," Murray explained. "There's no cure yet, though science is working on it."

"How come us campers don't get all these diseases that the counselors and workers get?" Ace asked.

"Well, you have to get shots before you come here, right?"

"Yeah."

"Okay, staff doesn't get shots."

"How come?"

"Because the state doesn't require it. I can't force them, can I? They'd have to pay out of their own pockets, of course. They're grown-ups who get to decide things for themselves — which, by the way, is one of the great things about this country. I might just write a letter on this to President Kennedy. People who work with children should be more sanitary. Surely the government could afford the shots."

That seemed to satisfy the Council of Elders. They went off to their new duties while Murray repaired to his office and drafted a letter on a Rexograph blank not to President Kennedy but to all Camp Timahoe parents explaining that Parents' Weekend would have to be postponed until August due to an outbreak of Rubella. Federal health officials had also declared an embargo on mail in Orleans County, Vermont, temporarily shutting the post offices, Murray added, to avert the spread of the disease. This would probably be the last situation report they would receive for ten days, he wrote.

Now it happened, under the new disposition of things, that Ace Greenaway was in the kitchen at 7:15 the next morning, preparing to set out the boxes of Corn Flakes, Shredded Wheat, Kix, and Raisin Bran as instructed. The adjoining dining room was still empty, since the campers were not responding to *Reveille* as crisply as they had pre-emergency. The cereal boxes happened to be in the mouse-proof cabinets beside a window that looked out over the driveway circle that the Lodge fronted upon. Ace watched a black Lincoln Continental car the size of a ferry-boat pull down the dusty driveway along the tennis court at what seemed an unusually rapid rate of speed. It stopped short in the turn-around with squealing brakes in a rooster tail of dust.

A tall, fat man got out. He was dressed in a shiny dark suit, skinny black tie, and sunglasses. He appeared to be uncomfortable in his clothing. He pulled his pants up to his bay window belly before slamming the car door shut. Ace noted that it was unusual to see Vermonters in business suits. He wondered if the man was an angry parent who had gotten wind of the difficulties afflicting Camp Timahoe, come to take his child back home.

Just then, a screen door slapped and Murray came into view striding across the

21

driveway circle to the big fat man in the suit. Ace noticed that they did not shake hands. Murray seemed to be talking strenuously, with a lot of hand gestures. The fat man leaned against his car, took something out of his pocket and buffed his nails while Murray talked at him. The fat man didn't even look at Murray. He seemed so absolutely relaxed leaning against the car that Ace was shocked to see him suddenly grab a fistful of Murray's shirt front and draw the Camp Timahoe director's face within inches of his own fat, jowly face. Murray appeared to go limp at that moment, like a helpless small animal in the grip of a meat-eating monster. Next, the fat man was smacking Murray about the head, still holding him by the shirt, and then he flung Murray down into the dust of the driveway and commenced to kick him.

    That was when Ace Greenaway grabbed a thirteen-inch cook's knife from the block on the counter, and raced through the separate kitchen door to the driveway brandishing the weapon.

    "Get offa him, you fat bastard!" Ace yelled.

    "Go back inside!" Murray yelled back from the ground.

    "Put that thing down before you hurt yourself, kid," the fat man said.

    "I'll stick it in your big fat belly if you hit him again," Ace said.

    The fat man sneered and hitched up his uncomfortable pants again. He issued a laugh of contempt and derision and opened the door of the big black car. Before he got in, he pointed at Murray and said, "Three days, pal. Three days!" Then he got behind the wheel, spun around the driveway circle with a great fanfare of flying gravel, and drove off the premises.

Murray hastened to get up and dust himself off. A trickle of blood ran out of his left nostril, and his left eye was red and swollen.

"Come with me, son," he said to Ace, and rather roughly dragged him inside the Arts and Crafts cabin next to the lodge. He told Ace to sit down on a stool beside a workbench where a dozen crude clay pinch-pots stood awaiting their turn in the kiln. The walls were adorned with tempera paintings of Little Big Woods Lake, copper bas-relief portraits of Indians, and lanyards-in-progress hanging from nails.

"I was just trying to help," Ace said.

"I know, son. Here, give me the knife."

"Don't send me home!"

Murray issued an ironic cackle.

"Don't worry about that, Ace," he said. He grabbed an old wash-rag streaked with dried clay and blew his nose in it. When he saw the blood, he said, "Ach!"

"Who was that man?" Ace asked.

"He was, uh, from the electric company. We're a little behind on the bill."

"Are they gonna shut it off in three days?"

"Not if I can help it," Murray said. He seemed to try to collect himself, sighing and sniffling. "Look, son, I appreciate you trying to defend my honor out there. The thing is, it would best if the other campers didn't know about this, uh, little incident. Can you do me a huge favor and keep it to yourself? It's important."

"I guess," Ace said. "Sure."

"Believe me, it would be best for all concerned."

"Your eye's getting all puffy and blue," Ace observed.

"It is?" Murray said. He rushed over to the door and looked at his reflection in the little two-over-two window there. "If anybody asks, say that I tripped over a hose."

From the arts and crafts cabin, they could hear the other campers moiling around in the nearby lodge dining room.

"I better go," Ace said. "I was just putting out the cereal."

"Right," Murray said. "They'll be hungry as wolf cubs. Remember, I tripped over a hose, is what you saw."

"Yeah. Okay."

"By the way, you can double up at the next candy canteen. We'll get through this, son. Don't you worry."

At supper, Ace received instructions to go sleep in Bunk 3 that night, where the erstwhile Werner had been counselor. Bunk 3 was the lowest intermediate bunk. The four boys there were seven years old. Next door in Bunk 4, Buddy Wollenreich had been put in charge. In the interval before Taps, Ace read to his young charges from the paperback novel, *Psycho*, by Robert Bloch, recently turned into a hit movie by Alfred Hitchcock. The little ones cowered docilely in their bedding with rapt attention. Next door, Buddy regaled the eight-year-olds with his repertory of sick jokes. Gales of laughter rocked the cabin. But so adrenalized were the boys by these gags about amputees, deaf mutes, midgets, and the assorted misbegotten, that Buddy could not get them settled in bed. The laughter turned to shrieking, bed-bouncing, and rafter-swinging, and eventually Buddy marched the worst offender, one Alan Zwanger of Madison, New Jersey, out into the center of the Intermediate Grove and found a couple of two pound rocks for him to hold to demonstrate the Iron Cross.

"This exercise was invented by Hitler himself," Buddy informed the boy. At first, Zwanger seemed to enjoy the challenge, but inside of five minutes he dropped the stones and was bawling in a heap on the ground, begging to be left alone. Meanwhile, Ace and several other seniors drafted for bunk duty came out of their cabins to see what the ruckus was about. Alan Hufnagel, sixteen, with biceps like picnic hams from doing pull-ups from the rafters, sauntered over to where Buddy loomed over the blubbering heap of Zwanger.

"What's the big idea, Buddy?"

"They won't quit cutting up."

"The Iron Cross isn't for little kids."

"Hey, it works."

Hufnagel bent down and quietly told the weeping Zwanger to go back inside, which he did.

"Hey...!" Buddy said.

"What are you, some kind of Nazi faggot sadist?" Hufnagel asked, shining his flashlight directly in Buddy's eyes.

"I dunno," Buddy said. He didn't know what a sadist was. "I'm not a faggot, anyway."

"Then do me a favor. Don't torture the little kids. You want the parents of these little twats suing Murray?"

"I dunno...."

"'Cuz he's in enough trouble, if you haven't noticed. He doesn't need to be sued by some asshole parent." Hufnagel smacked Buddy upside the head with medium force.

"Ow!"

"Hey, Huff," Ace said, to divert Hufnagel's attention and protect Buddy. "What kind of trouble is Murray in anyway? What the heck's going on around here lately?"

"I'm not sure," the older boy said. "Something to do with money, I think."

"Is Camp Timahoe going down the tubes? I heard they might cut off the electricity in three days."

"Oh, great," Hufnagel said. "When that happens this place will be a complete zoo."

As it happened, by an ominous coincidence having nothing to do with the fat man in the Lincoln Continental, the electricity went out the next day. The boys did not notice it that morning because the sun was shining brightly when they woke up and went to breakfast, nor at lunch at the cookout patch, where Murray boiled 144 frankfurters over a wood fire. Ditto supper, once again frankfurters. But they did notice at twilight, around 8:15 p.m. when they retired back to their bunks and the single bare bulbs that hung from the centers of each cabin would not turn on.

As it also happened, Murray soon swung around in his Ford Country Squire station wagon to the intermediate grove, where he announced a special emergency ration of candy canteen. He carried the stacked boxes of Mars Bars, Chuckles, Charleston Chews, Sugar Daddies, Bit o' Honeys, and Necco Wafers around to each cabin, and explained that the problem with the electricity was due to a freak accident on Highway 58 between Camp Timahoe and Lost Indian involving a tractor-trailer truck striking a relay box. The driver had been arrested for aggravated

willful negligent destruction of public property,
Murray added.

"When's the light coming back on?" asked
Martin Erlander, seven, one of the kids in Ace's
bunk.

"Don't know, son," Murray said. "Soon, I'm
sure."

"I want to go home," Martin said.

Murray put down his candy boxes on the
footlocker and sat on the end of Martin's bed
holding up his majestic eight-battery lantern,
which was almost as bright as the regular cabin
light.

"Aw, no you don't," he said tenderly. "Do
you know why they call this camp?"

"No."

"Because in the olden times when we first
came here, it was like camping out. There was no
electric. And they didn't even have good
flashlights back then. That's what we're going to
do for a few days now, until authorities get the
service back up. Camping out is fun! Right?
Didn't you go on the junior camp-out last year to
see the ice caves in New Hampshire?"

"Yeah?"

"Wasn't it fun?"

"It rained. We got all wet."

"Oh? Well, you're in a nice snug bunk
now, with a roof and a washroom. Tell you what:
you boys can have a half-hour for flashlight war.
Would you like that?"

"I guess," Martin said.

"Hey, Murray, who punched you in the eye?" asked the boy in the next cot, Charles "Froggie" Asperger.

"Nobody," Ace chimed in. "He tripped over a hose."

"That's right, son," Murray agreed. "Embarrassing, I admit, but true. All right, boys, try not to wear out those flashlight batteries and sleep tight."

The meal procedure changed somewhat the following day, at least for lunch and supper. Murray announced that the supply of frankfurters had run out, and he had been unable to get to the store at Lost Indian for more, but there were lots of other delicious things in the larder, he said, and they were going to have those instead. He brought more pots and pans to the cookout patch in a wheelbarrow along with many No. 10 cans of those camp-out favorites: Dinty Moore Beef Stew, Dinty Moore Meatball Stew, Mother's Brand Corned Beef Hash, Chef Boyardee Ravioli, B & M Pork and Beans, and jumbo boxes of Kraft Macaroni and Cheese, and allowed each bunk to take its pick of what they wanted to eat, and cook it themselves!

Now, it happened to be Thursday, the evening of the street dance in Lost Indian, and while the boys ate, Murray announced that he would be taking the senior green team into town, as promised, while the red team would "hold down the fort," referee a giant game of Capture the Flag on the ball-field, and then put the little ones to bed. The ten green team campers, including Ace and Goose, piled into the old army truck and soon departed for town.

It was just twilight when Murray parked in the lot behind the old whitewashed town hall. A crowd of teens had already gathered on the blocked-off street in front of Hapworth's Men's and Ladies' Clothing Store. Local disc jockey Delbert "Toots" Thomason of WLI-AM was testing the public address system on a flat-bed truck parked there. The loudspeakers emitted screeches and squawks. Minutes later the dulcet voice of Sam Cooke came over the air crooning *Having a Party*. The teens commenced hopping and twisting.

"This is nauseating," Ace said. "Let's see what's playing at the movies." He and Goose hoofed over to the old opera house cattycorner from the dance on the square. The opera house was a forbidding gothic heap of clapboard with peeling paint and an offset bell tower not altogether plumb after all the years. It looked to Ace a little like the house in *Psycho* where the mummy of Norman Bates's mother lived. The movie playing that week was *Panic in the Year Zero*, starring Ray Milland and Frankie Avalon, an atomic war saga. They went in.

An hour and a half later, they emerged blinking back onto the square, where night had fallen.

"Hey, look," Goose said, pointing at the streetlights. "The electric's back on here."

"Didn't you realize that when the movie came on?" Ace said.

"No." Goose said. "Why would I?"

"Movie projectors, stupid," Ace said. "You have to plug them in."

"Oh? Okay...."

"We better get back to the truck. Come on."

The DJ was playing the hit *Johnny Angel* by Shelly Fabares across the square and the teens were slow dancing. They cut across and stopped to watch the action for a couple of minutes.

"Hey, lookit," Goose said. "There's Holzinger!"

The teen-aged camper had his arms draped around the bosomy Suzanne Brunelle and they were slowly swaying back and forth to the music. When the song ended, she stepped onto her tiptoes and kissed him on the mouth.

"Wow, she's built all right!" Goose remarked.

"Come on. Don't stare like a moron."

The DJ started wrapping up the festivities. He plugged his sponsors, the local Buick Dealer, Clearasil cream for acne courtesy of your Rexall pharmacist, and Hudnut's Septic Tank Service, and switched off the PA system. The crowd dispersed. The other green team seniors all managed to make it back to the truck around the appointed time, customarily ten o'clock when the dance always ended. After waiting a quarter of an hour, there was no sign of Murray.

"Holzinger's not here either," Skurtz announced, after counting heads.

They waited another ten minutes.

"We better send out a search party," Skurtz, the senior senior, decided. "Gosdorfer, you stay here with the truck."

"Why me?"

"Why not you? It has to be somebody. If they come back you tell 'em we're out searching for 'em. The rest of you, fan out around town and find 'em!"

In the days before strip malls, chain stores, and fast food emporia, American towns, even modest-sized ones, were actually full of businesses, many of them catering to the hungry and thirsty. Lost Indian, with its paper mill, brass machining mill, and Shortleigh's Ice Creamery, not to mention the Vermont School of Vocations and Trades, had a network of downtown streets around the courthouse square that, besides the usual shops, contained many watering holes and restaurants for the various classes of citizens, the factory workers, the foremen and supervisors, the teachers of truck mechanics and plumbing, and the people who sat behind desks in ties and jackets.

Most of the boys followed Skurtz over to Main Street, which ran off the far side of the square. Ace ventured down the lesser Coolidge Street, which wound downhill to the Luxe Brass Casing Plant (estab. 1919) and the rail yard beside the Lamoille River. In the weak light of the street lamps, it had the flavor of the townscape depicted in *The Cabinet of of Dr. Caligari*, a horror movie of the silent era, all strange, jagged angles, with a blade-like sliver of moon carving through dark clouds above the jumble of rooftops. He passed Turnledge's Field and Stream Sports, the window of which was full of wonderful trout fly displays, wicker creels, shotguns, stuffed bass and pheasants, and then Oakum's confectionary with its tiered display of bon-bons, fruit jellies, coconut balls, and bricks of fudge. Both shops were closed at this hour on a weeknight. Next door to Oakum's was the Eight Point Bar, favored by brass workers. The swing-shift was just getting off and dozens of men hoisted beer glasses under the mounted deer head above the bar. Patsy Cline's hit, *Crazy*, played on the jukebox.

"Your daddy ain't here," a sinewy man with a missing eye tooth cracked as Ace stepped in looked around. The man's companions joined him in laughter.

Ace didn't see Murray anywhere at the bar and moved on.

Further down the street, past Charbonneu's Plumbing Supply, and Borchard's Record Shack was a drinking establishment called the Casting Pit. It, too, was the lair of factory workers, but of a lower order, men with sooty faces and filthy clothes, drinking quietly with a kind of medicinal concentration. No music played and the place smelled sour. Ace did an about-face and left.

Down a little further, he came to the Oasis Restaurant and Lounge. A neon sign propped up against a potted palm in the window said "Open." He ventured within. The place turned out to be a "nice" establishment with white tablecloths, and cushy banquette seating, and little electric lamps on each table. Exotic music with a lot of bent, flatted notes played lowly in the background. A man wearing a necktie lingered over drinks with a good-looking woman at one table from which their kebab and baklava plates and been bussed. When he glanced to his left, Ace was electrified to see Murray Horvath slumped at the bar with his head resting on his arms and a highball glass off to the side, the ice cubes melting into the remaining scotch and soda. A broad-featured, dark-haired man with a very thin mustache was polishing glasses behind the bar.

"Time to wake up," the man said in an exotic accent. "Boy is here to take you home."

"Huh," Murray raised his head, blinking. "'Nother round, Habib," he said.

"No, Mister. We close up now. You go with boy."

"Boy...?"

Murray's head swiveled. When his eyes took in Ace, the understructure of his whole face seemed to struggle to rearrange itself.

"What'r you doin' here, Ace?"

"It's late, sir. We've been waiting for you at the truck."

"Huh...?" Murray's eyelids started to flutter.

"We have to go back to camp."

"There is no camp," Murray said. His head dropped on the bar and he started sobbing into his elbows.

"Sure there is," Ace said. "We left it only a couple of hours ago."

"They took it away from me."

"He been like this all night," the bartender said. "Go home with boy, Mister!"

Ace was both frightened and mystified. The couple lingering at the dinner table got up and left, casting glances of disapproval at Ace and Murray on their way out

"The camp is still there, Murray. Come on, you'll see."

"Here, take these," Murray said, handing Ace a split-ring groaning with keys. "Mebbe Holzinger can drive."

"They can't find Holzinger."

"He'll turn up."

By now, Habib the bartender and owner of the Oasis came around to the patron's side of the bar and started to physically assist Murray off his stool.

"Boy will take you home now," he said. "Go."

Habib got Murray to his feet and all but shoved him out the door with Ace right behind. Murray wobbled and Ace propped him up. Habib locked the door to the Oasis behind them with an emphatic click and then the "Open" sign went dark.

"All right," Murray said, exhaling his resignation into the cool night air, "where'sa truck?"

"Up this way," Ace pointed. Murray put one foot in front of the other and shortly assumed a mode of locomotion that resembled walking. He used Ace's shoulder like the handle of cane as they wove and lurched up the deserted street.

"You know what the law of the jungle is?" he asked.

"It's God's law," Ace said. "Because humans don't rule in the jungle."

"Tha's right. It's eat or be eaten. The whole world is the jungle, son. God's law is rough stuff."

"God must be a Nazi."

"Yeah, I guess he kind of is," Murray agreed. "You boys are better than that."

"Yeah, we're not Nazis, anyway, except for Gosdorfer."

"I'm gon' miss all of you."

"We're still here, Murray. And Camp Timahoe will always be there. Don't you worry."

"If you say so."

Murray stopped in his tracks to blubber again, leaning on Ace, at the same time that Skurtz and three other green team seniors appeared further up the street in front of Turnledge's Field and Stream Sports.

"Hey, there they are!" one of them cried.

"You found 'im!" another said. "Yahoo!"

"Wow, he's a mess," Skurtz remarked when he got closer.

Soon they were all helping Murray get the rest of the way up the hill to the parking lot behind the town hall. The others had found Holzinger too, under a lilac tree in the town square, where he'd been making out with Suzanne Brunelle. They were both at the truck when Ace, Murray, and the rest got back to the parking lot.

"Wha' say, boys," Murray greeted the green team.

They didn't know what to say. They were not used to seeing their elders drunk.

"Maybe you'd like to ride in the back," Holzinger ventured.

"Yeah, I'd like that," Murray said. "Maybe one o'you can drive."

The seniors swapped glances all around. None of them volunteered.

"Anyone got a license?" Skurtz asked.

"I got the junior," Hufnagel said, "but you're not allowed to drive at night."

"I can drive," said Suzanne Brunelle.

The others appeared nonplussed.

"She can't come to camp," Skurtz said.

"We're eloping," Holzinger explained.

Murray's eyes had closed and his knees buckled. Ace and Hufnagel struggled to hold him up.

"Somebody fish the keys out of his pocket," Skurtz said.

"I already got 'em," Ace said and reluctantly handed them over to the stunning Quebecois maiden. Her father owned the Lost Indian lumber yard and she had made deliveries for him in a similar truck since she was thirteen, which was two years ago.

Murray roused himself briefly but needed assistance to get up into the back of the truck. The boys both pulled him from above and pushed him from behind, and soon he was sound asleep again under the left front bench seat

38

behind the cab. Holzinger sat beside Suzanne up front, hoping to receive some instruction about driving a Ford war surplus GT8A cargo truck. It took a while for her to find the right key among the many on the ring, but then the engine roared to life and soon Suzanne was shifting expertly through the gears as they left the lights of Lost Indian behind.

When they got back to camp at midnight, the green team helped Murray into his own cabin, a log house isolated from everything else behind the tennis courts, and deposited him on the sofa there with its motif of ducks on the wing. He was snoring loudly again before they finished raiding his refrigerator and left.

The intermediate grove of bunks, on the other hand, looked like a war zone. The game of capture the flag had apparently morphed into a pitched battle of all against all, with flashlights slicing through the night, and campers running madly around, and waterguns spritzing, and water balloons lobbed like grenades out of the darkness, and even some roman candles going off like mortar rounds. Ricky Gendelman, nominally in charge, had lost control completely. Holzinger , Skurtz, and Hufnagel were unable to influence anything. But Suzanne Brunelle stepped into the fray clapping her hands and shouting like a dominating Quebecois *maman*, and within half a minute the battle subsided and all the combatants slumped in place like prisoners of war. With her support, Holzinger and the others got the young ones back into their cabins, and administered head noogies to Gendelman and his feckless crew of red team seniors who had allowed things to degenerate so badly. By one in the morning, everyone was asleep, including Holzinger and his "bride-to-be" in the otherwise deserted Bunk 13.

With the electric out, there was no *Reveille* bugle over the loudspeakers the next morning and all the boys slept late. At quarter to nine, Ace Greenaway hurried up the hill by himself to the lodge to set out the breakfast cereal. Though hardly a master of logistics, he could tell that the three and a half boxes of cereal remaining would not be enough to feed all his fellow campers. On top of that, only one half gallon of milk was left in the walk-in refrigerator. He rooted out a cardboard silo of Quaker Oats from the pantry and began to follow the instructions for cooking it. But by the time he got the oats, water, and salt all measured in a large cook-pot, and put it on the stove, and tried to light the burner at least a dozen times, he realized that there was no more propane gas left in the tall silver tank that stood outside the kitchen wall like a drunken deep-sea diver. He was suffering a pang of personal failure in the discharge of his duties when, idly looking out the window, he saw a car pull into the circular drive. It was not a big black Lincoln Continental like last time but a bulbous, pastel green Volvo that looked like the cars in the old 1930s gangster movies. It rolled gently to a stop and the driver stepped out, a trim man in his forties wearing khaki pants and a tattersall shirt with a plastic pen shield in the pocket and tortoiseshell eyeglasses. The man did a 360-degree turn in place, as though he were trying to take in the entirety of Camp Timahoe in panorama. Ace hurried out the kitchen door to see who it was and what he wanted.

"Oh, hello there," the man said pleasantly. "Gosh, where is everybody?"

"They're... on a fire drill," Ace said.

"Huh...? Wouldn't they be lined up outside here somewhere?"

"They're lined up at the waterfront."

"How come all the way down there?"

"It's a forest fire drill."

"They have those here?"

"Yes sir, in Vermont they do," Ace assured him. "Can I do something for you?"

"Oh, well, I'm Alan Zwanger's dad. That is, he's my son. Do you know Alan Zwanger? He's a bit younger than you, of course, but—"

"Sure, I know Zwanger," Ace said. "He's having a great time here this summer. Just great. What a great kid. Say, didn't you get the letter that Murray sent out?"

"What letter?"

"About parents' weekend getting cancelled."

"No, I've been up in Labrador for several weeks," Mr. Zwanger said. In fact, he was a professor of Ornithology at Farleigh Dickenson College in Madison, New Jersey.

"Where's Labrador?

"Way up north in Canada. The wild and wooly seacoast."

"What's up there?"

"A particular bird I'm studying. The puffin."

"That's a bird?"

"Oh, a magnificent one."

"Sounds like a cereal."

"Here, I'll show you."

Mr. Zwanger went to the car to retrieve a book written, as it happened, by himself: *Courtship and Dominance Patterns of the Atlantic Puffin.* He opened to the frontispiece, a color plate of the bird, with its florid orange bill and mask-like face.

"Wow. Are you sure that's not a toy bird?" Ace said. "It looks like plastic."

Just then, a mixed band of a dozen campers, seniors, intermediates, led by Bob Skurtz, marched out the front door of the lodge.

"Hey Greenaway," Skurtz hollered. "Where the hell's our breakfast?"

"I was just getting it," Ace said.

More campers started pouring through the lodge door, as if the building were vomiting them out. Among them was Mr. Zwanger's son, Alan.

"Dad!" he cried, rushing across the driveway circle. "What are you doing here?"

"I was coming home from my field trip, son. Remember? I wanted to see the old place." As yet another matter of fact, Mr. Zwanger had attended Camp Timahoe himself as a child way back before the war, when the camp had just started. That was the principal reason that his son Alan had been sent to it. "Say, where's Murray, anyway?"

"He got shitfaced drunk last night," Alan said. "The place is going crazy. The counselors all quit and they're starving us to death. The seniors are Nazis!"

Mr. Zwanger laughed, remembering the wild things that boys liked to say after being away from the civilizing restraints of home for many weeks. But before he could ask his son anything else, a county sheriff's car with a revolving blue gumball light on its roof turned into the camp driveway, followed by a two-tone Chevy Bel Air with giant tailfins.

The two sheriff's deputies remained in the car a moment talking to headquarters on the radio. But a brawny man in denim and plaid with thick black hair combed straight back on his head popped out of the Chevy and angrily slammed the door. This would be one Hector Brunelle, owner of Lost Indian Lumber and father of the magnetic Suzanne. He marched straight over to Mr. Zwanger.

"You de fellow in charge?"

"No," Mr. Zwanger said forthrightly.

"Where my little girl is?" Brunelle demanded in his pronounced Quebecois accent.

Hufnagel, Skurtz, and several of the other boys pointed down the hill in the direction of the senior grove. Brunelle reared back, punched Mr. Zwanger in the nose, and loped off to where the boys had pointed. By now, the deputies had emerged from their battle wagon and helped Mr. Zwanger to his feet.

"You Mr. Horvath?" the shorter one asked.

"No, I'm Mr. Zwanger. Dr. Zwanger, actually. I'm just a parent."

"Do you know the whereabouts of Mr. Horvath?" the taller deputy asked.

"No," Dr. Zwanger said. "What's going on around here?"

"That's what we're here to find out," the short deputy said.

Meanwhile, Murray Horvath emerged on the footpath that wound through the pines behind the tennis court and strode manfully to the driveway circle. He looked pale but otherwise unimpaired.

"What's going on officer?" he asked the taller deputy.

"If you're Mr. Horvath, we were about to ask you the same thing," the shorter one said.

"I'm Horvath," Murray said. He seemed momentarily off balance. "Is that you Harvey? Harvey Zwanger?"

"Yes, it's me Murray," Dr. Zwanger said, dabbing at his bloodied nose with a handkerchief.

"Great to see you again," Murray said, seizing Dr. Zwanger's free hand and pumping it vigorously. "You know Alan's doing real well. He's a heckuva ballplayer — better than you ever were, heh heh — and he swims like a goshdarn bottlenose dolphin —

"Uh, Mr. Horvath," the tall deputy said. "There doesn't seem to be much adult supervision here."

"That's not true," Murray said. "Why, Harvey Zwanger's here, and I'm here and, heck, you two are here."

"This is a camp, right?" the short deputy said.

"A concentration camp," Alan Zwanger said.

"Heh heh," Murray said.

"Where are your people, sir?" the tall deputy asked.

"These are my people," Murray replied. "These red-blooded American boys, holding up the Camp Timahoe tradition of self reliance and rugged individualism. That right boys?"

45

Many of the younger ones piped right up, crying, "Yeah!" But Hufnagel and the older ones coughed, or turned their gaze skyward, or pretended to whistle a tune.

"Your staff," the short deputy said. "They're not here."

"They were here," Murray said, "but they're off duty now."

"All of them at once?" the tall deputy asked. "How can you—"

"Do you know what happened last night?" Murray interrupted him, stepping around Dr. Zwanger and facing the two deputies rather aggressively.

"What?"

"Marilyn Monroe committed suicide," Murray said.

The deputies swapped a glance.

"I had to give my staff the day off," Murray said. "They were devastated."

The short deputy went to his car and retrieved a clipboard from the seat.

"Sir, we have a writ from Judge Perkins in Lost Indian regarding foreclosure on this property per the St. Johnsbury Savings and Loan.

"Oh, that," Murray said. "That's the law of the jungle."

"No," the tall deputy said. "That's the law of the State of Vermont."

Just then, Hector Brunelle rounded the corner of the lodge porch with his daughter

Suzanne in tow, more or less, clutched awkwardly by a hank of her luxuriant dark hair. She was shrieking. The deputies, and indeed everybody present watched as he stuffed her in the back seat of his Chevy. He regarded the two law officers and Murray Horvath and even Dr, Zwanger with a look of contempt, shook his fists at them, and shouted a long stream of imprecations in the specially inflected French of his homeland.

"I think you better come with us, sir," the short deputy said to Murray.

"Do you fellows enforce the law of the jungle?" Murray asked.

"If that's what it is," the short deputy said. "Don't make us put the cuffs on you, sir."

"Very well," Murray said. "Can I just say a few words to my boys."

"Go ahead," the tall deputy said.

"But make it short," the short one said.

"Boys," Murray began, but he was interrupted.

"Is she really dead?" Goose asked.

"Who? Marilyn?" Murray said. "Apparently so,"

"Did she shoot herself in the head, like Hitler?" SB asked.

"No, I think it was pills, son. *Ahem*.... Boys, the bedrock of our Camp Timahoe traditions is fair play—"

"Why'd you do it Murray?" Ace asked vehemently, verging on tears.

"Do what?"

"Ruin the camp."

"I, uh. Well, son, the cost of everything went up and I borrowed money from the wrong people—"

"That's enough," the tall deputy said.

"Should cover it," the short one agreed. They grabbed Murray by either arm and jammed him into the backseat of their patrol car. He rolled down the window as the engine turned over and purred.

"I apologize for any inconvenience to your families," Murray shouted out the rear window as the car rounded the circle and headed back out to the road with Hector Brunelle's Chevy following in its plume of dust.

It was left to Harvey Zwanger to begin contacting the parents of the campers. Before the day was over, he also managed to charter a bus for the eight-hour trip back to Manhattan and a moving van to convey all the footlockers and belongings of the campers right behind it. Fortunately, Dr. Zwanger was heir to Smelzrite cat litter fortune — a circumstance that had allowed him to pursue his ornithological passions — and also enabled him to buy steak dinners for all seventy-three starving campers when the bus made a rest-stop at the Chez Fonfon restaurant on Route 5 outside Holyoke,

Mass., a place that he knew and loved from his many trips to the land of the Atlantic puffin.

Ace Greenaway said goodbye to his summer pals, the Four Horsemen of Campocalypse, with a special brand of sorrow that exceeded their partings of previous years, since he suspected that Camp Timahoe, like the fabulous Marilyn Monroe, had tragically ceased to exist. He was correct about that, though he did not know that he would spend the summer-yet-to-come in a weathered gray cottage by the sea on the enchanted Island of Nantucket, where the whale-fishes blow, and that he would have previously unimagined adventures there, some of them involving girls.

Now, it happened that Ace Greenaway's father, Robert Greenaway, like Dr. Harvey Zwanger, had been a Timahoe camper in the years before the war (they knew each other as boys, nicknamed respectively Flash and Birdy). It also happened that Robert "Flash" Greenaway was an attorney with the estimable New York firm, Slather Bancroft Hooker & Feigenbaum. His affection for Camp Timahoe and its founder was such that he made a number of phone calls that got the sore beset Murray Horvath out of the tiny jail in Lost Indian. Subsequently he managed to restructure the camp's debt in such a way that Murray regained possession of the property. Having started out as a prosecutor in the US

Attorney's office, Flash also knew his way around the loan-sharking world, and a few more phone calls resulted in two US marshals paying a call on the house of one Carmine "Fancy Pants" Gasolino in Bay Ridge, Brooklyn, who agreed to forgive a certain loan booked to one M. Horvath in exchange for dismissal of charges for transporting known prostitutes across state lines.

Finally, it happened that Murray Horvath had lost his taste for the summer camp business. But in one of those ironies of history, he started a new venture on the property manufacturing a piece of wooden outdoor furniture that would become a prized fixture of New England summers for decades to come: the Lost Indian Lawn Lounger. He set up a small factory in the old camp lodge building where the Brothers of the Practical Arts had long ago crafted their Lumbar Hygiene Recliner, and, in fact, Murray's chair owed a lot design-wise to that sadly forgotten gem. He also took advantage of a state program that sent him parolees from the Vermont State Penitentiary on work-release, and was actually paid by the state to employ them at chair-making. The revenue allowed him to winterize all the former camp bunks and install wood-burning stoves in each, where the parolees would spend some of the happiest moments of their otherwise tortured and hapless lives.

Ace Greenaway — once again known as Jeff — spent the remaining weeks of August under circumstances he had once regarded as unthinkable: on the steamy isle of Manhattan with its glaring pavements and pointless bustle. Luckily, his arrival coincided with a twelve-day home-stand of the American League-leading Yankees. His parents felt sorry enough for him and his aborted camp season that they gave him the requisite four dollars a day needed for a subway ride up to the Stadium, admission to the bleachers, and a two hot-dog lunch for the entire home-stand. By the time it was over, he was ready to begin his career at Ponsonby Hall, a private boarding school for boys deemed to be "thriving indifferently in the trenches of public education," as the catalog put it.

Made in the USA
Middletown, DE
14 June 2018